DINOSAUR COVE™

LOST IN THE JURASSIC

by
REX STONE

illustrated by
MIKE SPOOR

Series created by
Working Partners Ltd

OXFORD
UNIVERSITY PRESS

Special thanks to Jan Burchett and Sara Vogler

For Samuel Stephen Dyche R.S.

For Kate Adams for your creative imput
during my Jurassic times M.S.

OXFORD
UNIVERSITY PRESS

Great Clarendon Street, Oxford OX2 6DP
Oxford University Press is a department of the University of Oxford.
It furthers the University's objective of excellence in research, scholarship,
and education by publishing worldwide in

Oxford   New York

Auckland   Cape Town   Dar es Salaam   Hong Kong   Karachi
Kuala Lumpur   Madrid   Melbourne   Mexico City   Nairobi
New Delhi   Shanghai   Taipei   Toronto

With offices in

Argentina   Austria   Brazil   Chile   Czech Republic   France   Greece
Guatemala   Hungary   Italy   Japan   Poland   Portugal   Singapore
South Korea   Switzerland   Thailand   Turkey   Ukraine   Vietnam

Oxford is a registered trade mark of Oxford University Press
in the UK and in certain other countries

British Library Cataloguing in Publication Data

Data available

ISBN: 978-0-19-278990-7

1 3 5 7 9 10 8 6 4 2

Printed in Great Britain
Paper used in the production of this book is a natural,
recyclable product made from wood grown in sustainable forests
The manufacturing process conforms to the environmental
regulations of the country of origin

FACT FILE

➡️ JAMIE'S DAD'S MUSEUM ON THE BOTTOM FLOOR OF THE LIGHTHOUSE IN DINOSAUR COVE IS THE SECOND BEST PLACE IN THE WORLD TO BE. THE FIRST IS DINO WORLD, OF COURSE, WHERE JAMIE AND HIS BEST FRIEND, TOM, CAN VISIT THE JURASSIC ERA AND SEE REAL, LIVE DINOSAURS! BUT THE THING ABOUT VISITING DINO WORLD IS THAT YOU ARE SUPPOSED TO BE ABLE TO COME BACK...

JAMIE

- FULL NAME: JAMIE MORGAN
- AGE: 8 YEARS
- SIZE: 1 JATOM*
- TOP SPEED: 10 KPH
- LIKES: FOSSIL HUNTING AND LEARNING ABOUT DINOSAURS
- DISLIKES: BEING STUCK INDOORS

Jamie's eye

Jamie's foot

Jamie's hand

*NOTE: A JATOM IS THE SIZE OF JAMIE OR TOM: 125 CM TALL AND 27 KG IN WEIGHT

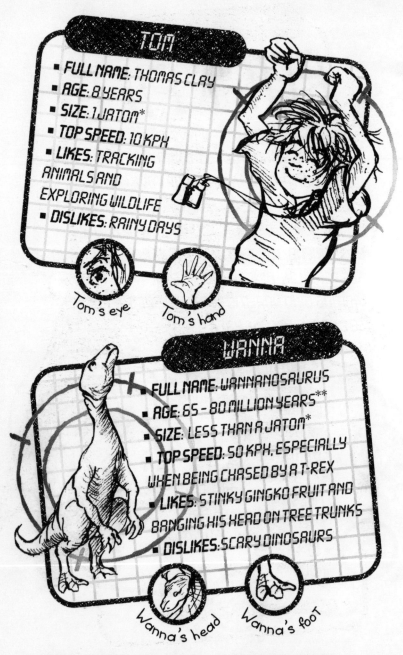

TOM

- **FULL NAME:** THOMAS CLAY
- **AGE:** 8 YEARS
- **SIZE:** 1 JATOM*
- **TOP SPEED:** 10 KPH
- **LIKES:** TRACKING ANIMALS AND EXPLORING WILDLIFE
- **DISLIKES:** RAINY DAYS

Tom's eye

Tom's hand

WANNA

- **FULL NAME:** WANNANOSAURUS
- **AGE:** 65 – 80 MILLION YEARS**
- **SIZE:** LESS THAN A JATOM*
- **TOP SPEED:** 50 KPH, ESPECIALLY WHEN BEING CHASED BY A T-REX
- **LIKES:** STINKY GINGKO FRUIT AND BANGING HIS HEAD ON TREE TRUNKS
- **DISLIKES:** SCARY DINOSAURS

Wanna's head

Wanna's foot

*NOTE: A JATOM IS THE SIZE OF JAMIE OR TOM: 125 CM TALL AND 27 KG IN WEIGHT
**NOTE: SCIENTISTS CALL THIS PERIOD THE LATE CRETACEOUS

PTEROSAUR

Pterosaur's Tail

Pterosaur's claw

Pterosaur's Teeth

Pterosaur's eye

- **FULL NAME:** PTEROSAUR – MEANS WINGED LIZARD
- **AGE:** 65 – 220 MILLION YEARS
- **LENGTH:** UP TO 14 JATOMS*. FROM THE SIZE OF A BAT TO THE SIZE OF AN AEROPLANE
- **WEIGHT:** UP TO 5 JATOMS*
- **LIKES:** HEIGHTS
- **DISLIKES:** BIGGER PREDATORS

*NOTE: A JATOM IS THE SIZE OF JAMIE OR TOM: 125 CM TALL AND 27 KG IN WEIGHT

DINOSAUR COVE

Village

Marina

Sealight Head

8

Landslips where
clay and fossils are

High Tide beach line

Low Tide beach line

DINO CAVE

Smuggler's Point

Sea

CHAPTER 1

'Check out that massive fossil!' exclaimed
Jamie Morgan as he stared at the picture of
the huge dinosaur bone on the poster in front
of him. 'That must have been some dino!'

Jamie's dad had just put up a new display
in the museum on the ground floor of their
lighthouse home. It was all about the first
discovery of the dinosaurs.

His best friend Tom Clay nodded. 'This
megalosaurus thigh bone was dug up over
three hundred years ago,' he read. 'Wow!

No one knew dinosaurs existed then. It says here that people thought it was the bone of an ancient giant human.'

'We know that's not true,' said Jamie. 'But wouldn't it have been cool if it was?'

Tom strode up and down between the exhibit cases, swinging his arms fiercely. 'Here comes Tom the Prehistoric Giant ready to take on all attackers.'

'He wouldn't have stood a chance against Jamie the Jurassic Megalosaur,' declared Jamie, raising his hands like claws and charging after him.

'We'll see about that!' boomed Tom in his deepest voice. 'I'll just uproot a handy tree and whack you over the head.' He swung the pretend weapon at Jamie, who was roaring and snapping at his enemy.

'Mind my exhibits!' laughed Mr Morgan as he went by with Jamie's grandad, carrying boxes to the museum office.

Jamie took another look at the poster and lowered his voice. 'You know, our secret Dino World would be very different if humans had been around all that time ago.'

MODEL DINOSAURS

ARM BONES

SKULLS

FRAGILE

AMMONITES

LEG BONES

'But we like it the way it is,' replied Tom firmly. 'Just us and the dinosaurs.'

Jamie and Tom had discovered the hidden entrance to a world of living dinosaurs in the back of a secret cave. No one else knew that the two friends sneaked off to Dino World for amazing prehistoric adventures.

'Come and look at the news, boys!' Jamie's grandad called. 'You're not going to believe what this scientist has found.'

Jamie and Tom ran into the office, where his dad and grandad were gazing at the TV on the wall. Grandad handed over a bag of

FRAGILE

toffees for Jamie and Tom to snack on
while they watched.

A reporter was standing outside a cave,
holding out his microphone to a fierce
looking man in a hat.

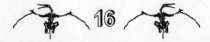

'Are you sure you haven't made a
mistake, Professor Jenkins?' the
reporter was saying.

'I'm certain,' insisted the
scientist, looking intently at
the camera. 'The world
may not be ready for

this discovery but I'm telling you that human beings lived as long ago as the Jurassic era.'

Jamie and Tom gawped at the screen.

'It can't be true, can it, Dad?' Jamie asked his father, with a worried glance at Tom.

Mr Morgan laughed. 'He must have got it wrong,' he said. 'There's never been any evidence.'

'Could you show us the proof that backs up your claim?' the reporter asked the professor.

'I have it right here,' answered the professor, 'trapped millions of years ago in this piece of amber.'

He held up the transparent orange amber. The camera zoomed in on it. Embedded deep inside was a small white tooth.

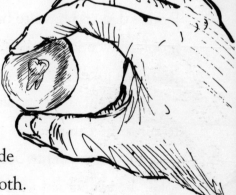

'And you claim this is a human one!' said the reporter.

'Indeed it is!' replied the professor. 'We found it in Jurassic rock. Once we extract DNA from this tooth, we shall be able to prove that early humans really did live two hundred and fifty million years ago.'

Jamie's grandad shook his head. 'It's all poppycock,' he muttered.

Jamie turned to his dad. 'Imagine if it was true and you had to reorganize the whole museum!'

'Don't even think about it!' laughed Jamie's dad. 'I'd have to have much more proof. Maybe someone's put that tooth in resin as a joke.'

The scientist was now holding a box up towards the camera.

Tom gasped. 'That doesn't look like a joke!' he exclaimed.

Lying in the box was what looked like a fossilized human hand!

The reporter stared hard into the camera. 'This is a most amazing discovery. Experts will

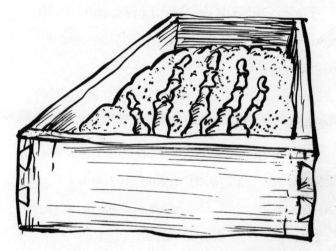

be examining these finds this very afternoon. Tune in for an update at four o'clock.'

Mr Morgan grinned at Jamie and Tom. 'Don't look so worried, boys. We won't be turning the museum upside down yet. There'll be another explanation for those fossils.' He switched the TV off. 'If there were humans

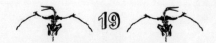

at the time of the dinosaurs scientists would
have found evidence of them long before now.
After all, they've been digging up dino bones
for three hundred years.'

'We're going to do a bit of research on this
ourselves,' said Jamie, catching Tom's eye.
'See you later.'

'Make sure you're back by four,' called
Grandad. 'That reporter chappy said
there'll be more news on the tooth then.'

'We will!' yelled the boys.

The boys dashed from the
office.

'This is terrible!' whispered
Tom when they were out of earshot.
'What if those remains really are
human? We've never seen any signs of
human beings in our parts of the Jurassic.'

'I reckon Dad's right,' muttered Jamie,
thinking it out. 'There can't have been people

living all that time ago . . . so there's only one
other explanation of the scientist's find.'

'Maybe we're not the only ones to have
found a way into Dino World,' gasped Tom.

'It has been a long time since we've been
to the Jurassic,' said Jamie.

'What if someone's been and
everything's changed?' Tom
wondered.

Jamie looked at him
in horror. 'If other humans
have been there . . .'

' . . . they might not keep it
quiet,' finished Tom. 'Everyone
would know about our secret world.'

'Tourists would come and trample all
over it,' said Jamie, 'and I bet the scientists
wouldn't leave it alone.'

'Come on,' said Tom. 'We've got to go to
Dino World and see what's going on.'

CHAPTER 2

Jamie swung his backpack on to his
shoulder and the two boys scrambled up
the rough rocky path from Muddy Beach to
Smuggler's Point. Once inside the dark cave
high in the cliff, Jamie took out his torch
and crawled through the smaller cave at
the back, where a row of fossilized dinosaur
footprints led to the far wall. Then he
hesitated.

'What's up?' asked Tom. 'We haven't
forgotten anything, have we?'

Jamie shook his head. 'Compass, Fossil Finder—and I picked up a Jurassic ammonite as we left, so we'll go back to the right time period. And I've got the toffees Grandad gave us if we get hungry.'

'Then what are we waiting for?' asked Tom.

'I've been thinking,' said Jamie. 'If other people have found a way into Dino World they might have broken the magic that takes *us* there. We'd never be able to pass through that wall again.' He gulped.

'We won't find out until we try,' said Tom. 'But we must be careful. If there are people there, they might not want us around.'

'You're right.' Jamie nodded. 'We mustn't be seen by anyone else.'

'I've just thought of something even worse,' said Tom. 'If they're not friendly, Wanna might not be safe.'

They stared at each other in the gloomy light. Every time they went to Dino World they met their little wannanosaurus friend.

He was a Cretaceous dinosaur but he was a part of the magic of Dino World and he came on all their adventures.

'We can't let anything happen to Wanna!' Jamie said fiercely as he placed his feet in the footprints.

Jamie usually felt a tingling rush of excitement every time he and Tom went on a new prehistoric adventure.

But today was different.

His stomach felt tight with anxiety. The future of Dino World might depend on them.

One . . . two . . . three . . . four . . . FIVE . . .

The boys counted aloud as they stepped towards the craggy rock wall. With a flash of light the wall vanished. They followed the dinosaur prints, which were now fresh and muddy, through Gingko Cave and out into the steaming heat of the Jurassic world. All about them, giant insects flew in and out among the huge trees of the jungle.

'I know we've got a serious mission, but it's great to be back in the Jurassic,' sighed Jamie.

'And there are no fresh human footprints,' said Tom, scanning the ground. 'So no one's come in this way—at least not recently.'

'Phew,' said Jamie. 'Next we've got to make sure Wanna—OOOF!'

Something small and heavy suddenly bowled into him, knocking him off his feet.

Grunk! Grunk!

'Wanna!' yelled Tom. 'You're OK!'

'That's great,' puffed Jamie, trying to stop the excited little wannanosaurus from licking his face completely off.

'We've got a mission, Wanna,' Tom told him as his friend struggled to his feet. 'Want to come with us?'

'Try and stop him.' Jamie laughed, as Wanna galloped round and round their feet. 'Let's think—we need to get to a good vantage point of Dino World.'

Tom got out his compass. 'If we go north we'll be heading through the jungle,' he said.

'We could find a tall tree and look out over the Plains,' suggested Jamie.

With Wanna scampering at their heels, they ploughed through the ferns and pushed

aside creepers that hung between the dense
trunks. After a while the little dinosaur began
to nudge their legs, almost tripping them up.

'I know what you want,' said Tom.
'Gingkoes. And I think I can see some
coming up.'

SQUAARRRK!

An ear piercing sound split the air.
The boys instinctively dived behind a rock.
'What's that?' gasped Tom, peering out.
The leaves of the nearby trees swayed
violently. The next second a group of

 31

towering dinosaurs had burst into view.
The boys could see a forest of tall, stout legs
stomping about, and long necks craning to
reach the gingko fruit in the branches above.

'We're lucky,' said Jamie. 'They're
herbivores.'

'They're awesome,' said Tom, as the gigantic bodies barged each other for the best fruit. Their young dived for anything that dropped to the ground.

Jamie whipped out his Fossil Finder. He muttered as he tapped in the key words. *'JURASSIC. LONG NECK, LONG TAIL . . .'*

'A single sharp claw on each foot . . .' added Tom.

'SMALL HEAD, BLUNT SNOUT . . .'

In an instant, the Fossil Finder knew the answer. 'They're camarasaurs,' Jamie said. *Grunk! Grunk!*

Wanna dashed in amongst the huge beasts,
making a lunge for every gingko that fell to

the ground. But the young cammies always
got there first.

Their little friend suddenly put his head
down and pawed the ground.

'Uh oh,' said Jamie. 'Wanna's going to try
and shake a gingko down just like he does to
the trees. He's about to ram the cammies!'

'No, Wanna!' shouted Jamie. 'You'll upset dino dinnertime.'

Wanna paused for a moment and watched the boys curiously, but kept looking back towards the cammies' legs. 'We'll have to lure him away before he causes a stampede,' Tom said. 'And there's only one thing that's sure to work—a personal supply of his favourite stinky snack.'

He crept out from his hiding place and made for an overhanging branch laden

with orange gingko fruit. He quickly picked a handful but as he turned back he found himself face to face with a baby cammie bending down to inspect him. Tom gulped as the baby cocked its head and looked at him with big wide eyes. He held out a gingko and felt the young dinosaur's slobbery nose in his palm as it snatched its snack and ambled off.

Tom took his chance and dashed back to join Jamie.

Grunk!

Wanna barged into him, pinning him to a tree. He turned to see the little dinosaur glaring at him.

Jamie laughed. 'Wanna came over as soon as he saw you feeding the cammie. He thinks all gingkoes should be for him.'

'I'd rather feed him than a three metre high baby dino,' said Tom. 'Here you are, Wanna. We'll take the rest for later.'

While Wanna gobbled his snack, Tom picked up a fallen leaf and wrapped the rest of the smelly fruit in it. Wanna grunked round him, hoping for another treat.

'Give me your backpack, Jamie,' said Tom. 'I'll hide these in it before our greedy little friend gets hold of them.' Jamie passed it to him and Tom stowed the package inside. He grabbed the toffees. 'Want one?' he asked.

'Oh, yes please,' replied Jamie. 'Wanna's had his treat so we can have one too.'

Tom popped
one into his mouth
and handed a couple to
Jamie. 'I'll take the backpack
for a while.' He swung it on to
his shoulder.

Jamie peered ahead. 'That
looks a good tree to climb,'
he said. 'I bet we'll be able to
see for miles from the top.'
He set off, chewing as he went.

Tom and Wanna caught
him up at the base of a
towering gingko tree.

Jamie grinned. 'Race
you to the top.'

The boys scrambled
up the enormous tree.
The thick, gnarly
branches made easy

footholds and they were soon high among
the leaves. Wanna grunked anxiously as his
friends disappeared from sight.

'Beat you!' declared Jamie at last. He was
clinging to a swaying branch above Tom's head.

'Not fair,' laughed Tom, pulling himself up
to join him. 'I had the backpack weighing me
down.'

Jamie grinned. 'I still won.' He pushed
aside the leaves in front of him. 'Wow! This is
such a great view.'

The boys stared out in awe at Dino World
spread before them. The dense jungle
covered all the nearby hilly land and below
it the Plains stretched away until it met the
volcanic peaks in the far distance.

Tom grasped the trunk
firmly with his legs and
pulled his binoculars out of
the backpack. He scanned
the Plains, from the
Massive Canyon in the

west right across to the sparkling river
in the east.

'What's that?' said Jamie, pointing to
a cloud of dust over by the Humongous
Waterfall. 'Is it people?'

Tom swung his binoculars on the scene.
'It's OK,' he said in relief. 'It's just dinosaurs.'

Tom passed the binoculars to Jamie so he
could see that it was an allosaurus attacking
two stegosaurs. The steggies were putting
up a good defence. The boys could hear the
angry roars of the huge beasts right across the

45

Plains. High in the air above the fight, a pair of pterosaurs were circling like vultures.

Tom pretended to talk to an imaginary camera. 'Tom Clay reporting from the top of a tree on an important dino mission.'

Jamie chuckled. Tom wanted to be a wildlife reporter when he grew up and he took every chance to practise.

'An awesome allosaurus has taken on two plucky stegosaurs,' Tom went on. 'He wants his lunch—they want to stay alive. It's a fierce fight. One thing's for certain, the pterosaurs hovering overhead are waiting to feast on whoever loses.'

The boys watched as the allosaurus clamped its jaws on the neck of one of its prey. Then it staggered back as the other stegosaurus gave it a thump with its armoured tail.

'They're evenly matched, viewers,' reported Tom. 'Hard to tell who's going to

 46

win this fight. Meanwhile, the pterosaurs
have given up on their steggie lunch. They're
coming this way. Looks like they're checking
out the trees.'

'I'm glad Wanna's safely hidden below,'
said Jamie. 'Those claws look vicious.'

'I think the allosaurus has had enough,'
said Tom. 'He's making a lot of noise but he's
moving away.'

'Time to get on with our search then,' said
Jamie.

'Let's go,' Tom replied. 'That professor said
the fossils were found in the mountains.'

'Then we should make for the Misty Mountains,' answered Jamie, 'and check out as much as we can.'

Suddenly a huge shadow fell over the boys.

'Watch out!' shouted Jamie.

CAAAW!

A sharp cry split the air and with it the beat of thick, leathery wings. One of the gigantic pterosaurs was swooping down towards Tom.

Tom yelped with terror as the huge creature's talons seized his arm in a vicelike grip and ripped him from the tree. The other pterosaur caught Tom's flailing leg in its sharp claws.

Horrified and helpless, Jamie watched as the two predators carried his friend up into the air and away over the jungle.

CHAPTER 4

Jamie scrambled down from the tree, making a huge jump to the ground in his hurry to follow the pterosaurs. The flying lizards with their dangling catch were now tiny dots in the distant sky. He started to sprint after them towards the Misty Mountains.

Grunk!

Wanna belted along beside him, looking around as if puzzled that Tom hadn't appeared from the gingko tree. They slashed their way through the ferns and spiky bushes. Jamie

could feel his chest heaving as he sucked in air but he had to keep going.

Tom was in terrible danger. If he didn't find a way to help him, his best friend was going to be pterosaur lunch! A dreadful thought hit him. Supposing it was *Tom's* fossilized hand that the scientist had found!

'That's not going to happen,' he panted to himself through gritted teeth. 'I'm going to rescue him.'

Wanna suddenly stopped and began to snuffle about in the

undergrowth.
He looked up,
squashed
gingko fruit
pulp all over
his nose.

Jamie skidded
to a halt. 'There isn't time for
snacking!' he urged. 'We've got to
find out where Tom's been taken.'

Grunk!

Wanna's call sounded urgent.

'Come on, boy,' coaxed Jamie, trying
to fight down his panic. 'We've got to go.
They're getting away. You can have some nice
gingkoes later.'

But the little wannanosaurus bounded up
to him and gave him a nudge, making Jamie
stumble downhill.

'What are you doing?' Jamie demanded.

Wanna licked his sticky snout and pushed
Jamie again. Then he darted forwards and
snaffled up another smashed gingko.

Gingkoes? thought Jamie. Something
wasn't right about what he was seeing but he
couldn't quite pinpoint what it was.

'This isn't helping Tom,' he said out loud.
'You can stuff your face if you want, Wanna.
I'm not waiting.'

Wanna didn't look up. He'd trotted on and found another squashed snack, this time under a clump of ferns.

Jamie peered up through the trees, searching desperately for a sight of the pterosaurs. And then he realized what had bothered him. He was standing amongst cycads and tall spiky conifers. There wasn't a single gingko tree to be seen in this part of the jungle. So where was Wanna finding the stinky fruits?

Then the answer came to him.

Tom!

'Tom!' he yelled, punching the air. 'It has to be.'

Somehow Tom must have managed to take the gingkoes out of the backpack and drop them as he was whizzed through the air. He was leaving a trail for them to follow. He'd known Wanna wouldn't be able to resist his favourite food. Jamie felt his spirits lifting.

'I'm sorry, boy,' he called, running over to join his dino friend. 'You were heading

in the right
direction all
along. Lead
the way.'

Grunk!

Following his nose
like a bloodhound,
Wanna scampered off
into a patch of tall
pointed horsetail ferns,
eagerly ferreting out
another gingko and
slurping it up. Then he
scampered off again down
the forested slope.

Jamie followed,
scattering a flock of bright
blue archaeopteryx who
gave shrill, startled cries
as they rose into the air.

Soon Jamie and Wanna had left the jungle and were out on the huge Plains. A herd of diplodocuses were grazing in the distance. Even in his panic to keep chasing after Tom, Jamie

couldn't help thinking how awesome they were, stretching their long necks up to the tall trees.

Wanna dashed towards yet another fruit, splattered all over a low rock. He gulped it

down and raised his head, looking to see where his next treat was.

'Even I saw that one,' laughed Jamie.

He patted the eager little dinosaur on his domed head.

'I never thought that your love of those stinky things would come in so useful. You'll be able to lead us to Tom!'

CHAPTER 5

Far away, high above the Plains, Tom was being sped towards the mountains. The wind buffeted his face, making his eyes stream. But much worse was the pulling and stretching of his arm and leg, clamped tightly in the pterosaurs' claws.

The land rose up now on either side. The pterosaurs made for a narrowing valley, dragging Tom through the top branches of the trees that filled the steep sides. Far below him a river raced back down towards the swampy jungle.

I have to get my bearings, he thought to himself as the branches scratched and scraped at his trailing leg. *So I can find my way back if they ever put me down.*

The sides of the valley were becoming steep cliffs.

'Whoah!' he cried as the pterosaurs suddenly plummeted in the air, twisting and turning. His arm felt as if it was being pulled out of its socket. One of the flying lizards shifted its grip and he nearly fell. He reached up with his other hand and clutched the scaly leg tightly.

What was going on? Then he heard a fierce screech and saw another pterosaur bearing down on them. His captors answered with angry squawks but the rival kept on coming. It snapped at their wings and then at Tom.

Uh oh, he thought desperately. *They're squabbling over who's going to eat me.*

Whoosh!

Suddenly in front of him a sheer cliff face loomed up. The pterosaurs weren't looking where they were going. He was going to be dashed against hard rock. With a horrible wrench to his ankle, they turned away at the last second.

But this had brought them back in the path of the other flying lizard. It snapped again at Tom. He kicked out hard at the cruel beak and knocked it aside. The attacking pterosaur scrabbled desperately with its claws, catching his backpack and nearly pulling it off. Tom tugged at it. There were things inside too precious to lose.

'You're not having that!' he yelled and yanked it free.

The pterosaur was wheeling around in the air, getting ready for another attack. But it seemed that Tom's captors weren't going to wait for that. They whizzed down, straight at the cliff. Tom could see the rock hurtling towards him again.

Just when he thought he really was going to be splattered this time, they changed their course and flew upwards, close to the cliff. Then the pterosaurs let go of him!

He tumbled through
the air . . . and landed
with a thud on a
hard ledge.

He scrambled up to
a sitting position and
peered out. His captors
were swooping after their
rival, screeching loudly.

'Now where am I?'
he muttered to himself.

He had been deposited
on a rock shelf in the foothills of the Misty
Mountains. He could see the Plains and
the forest beyond a short way down the
valley. Next to him was a pile of branches
and leaves. He peeked
into it and saw
five massive
eggs.

His heart sank. *This is the pterosaurs' nest and I'm definitely on the menu.*

'Not if I can help it,' he said aloud.

The first thing he had to do was complete his gingko trail. He couldn't see any sign of Jamie and Wanna but he hoped desperately they were somewhere in the trees, making their way along the valley towards him. He decided to drop another gingko right over the edge for them to find. He rummaged inside his backpack.

There was just one left. Tom watched it plummet and land *splat!* on the rocky ground far below.

Now he'd done all he could to help his friends find him. He hoped it was enough. He sat on the ledge, anxiously scanning the air for the return of the pterosaurs.

splat!

CHAPTER 6

'We've almost reached the Misty Mountains,' panted Jamie as he and Wanna sprinted across the dry, dusty Plains. 'Tom's got to be there somewhere.'

From the edge of the Plains he scoured the tree-covered valley that led to the mountain foothills. The fast flowing river came down from it and wound away to the east.

Grunk!

Wanna disappeared among the cycads and pines. Jamie ran in after him and caught

up just as the
little dinosaur was
gobbling down another gingko.

'I'm glad you don't get tired of your
favourite food,' said Jamie. 'I'd never be able
to follow Tom's trail on my own.'

They set off between the dense trunks,
Wanna with his snout to the ground.

BOOM! BOOM!

A deep, sinister sound made them stop in
their tracks.

BOOM! BOOM! BOOM!

The ground was shaking under their
feet. The next instant a huge dinosaur had
burst out into a clearing ahead. It stomped

heavily along on
its two back legs, head
whipping this way
and that, its slavering
jaws full of razor-sharp teeth.

Jamie steered Wanna to safety
behind a broad-trunked tree.

'Don't move, boy,' he
whispered. 'That's one
massive monster—and it
looks hungry.'

The towering dinosaur
barged among the trees,
raising its snout now and
again as if it could smell
something good to eat.
Jamie could see it was a
fighter—it had battle
scars all over
its body.

'Ferocious ten metre long dino,' he muttered to himself, 'bigger than an allosaurus, gigantic back legs, serrated teeth of a carnivore, bumps above the eyes. I may not have the Fossil Finder but I'm guessing that's a megalosaurus.' He gasped as the dinosaur avidly sniffed the air. 'We're in trouble, Wanna. It's a nasty predator and it's got our scent.'

The megalosaurus was slowly heading their way, flattening bushes and crunching branches as it approached. They could hear its heavy, snorting breath. Peeping through the leaves, Jamie could see its battered, scarred face.

*I've
only got a
few seconds
before it's
got us,* he
thought.

His eyes
swept the
ground and
fell upon a hairy,
coconut-like fruit. Very
slowly he bent and picked it up.

'No, Wanna,' he warned in a low voice as
the eager little dino tried to take a bite of it.
'It's all we've got to distract the megalosaurus.'

Jamie wished Tom was here. Escaping from
scary dinosaurs was much easier with a friend.
But he took a deep breath and hurled the
furry ball as far as he could manage, but it only
made it to a tree trunk a few metres away.

Jamie
held his
breath as the
megalosaurus swung its
head in the direction of the
tree and took two steps towards
it. But after a few sniffs, the beast
turned back towards Jamie and Wanna.
That almost worked, Jamie thought.
I've just got to throw it further away.

The dinosaur was just a few steps away
from where they were hiding. Jamie had
to act fast. He spotted two young saplings
growing close to each other, just over his
head. He quietly reached up and tied the
flexible tops together in a knot. 'This is going
to be a catapult,' he whispered to Wanna who
watched with his head cocked.

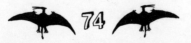

ROAR!

Jamie's whisper wasn't quiet enough. It had attracted the dinosaur's attention. Its beady eyes were fixed on their hiding place.

Jamie quickly placed the fruit at the top
and bent the saplings back as far as he could,
straining with the effort.

'This had better work!' he muttered as he
let go. The young trees whipped up, sending
the fruit sailing through the air, high over the

giant dino's head. It crashed down through
the branches behind the slavering
creature. Its sharp ears picked
up the sound immediately.
It shot round with a
rumbling cry and set
off to follow it.

Jamie punched the air in delight. 'It's sent him in the opposite direction to where we want to go. And we're not going to be here when he comes back. Find some more of Tom's clues, Wanna.'

The little wannanosaurus didn't need telling twice. He galloped off into the thick undergrowth of the valley, nosing out the trail of gingkoes. Jamie followed, trying to keep his eager friend in sight as he scampered ahead following the path of

the river. He stopped to listen now and again
but there were no heavy footsteps
coming their way.
At last the trail led
them away from the
river towards a sheer
rock face.

Grunk!

Wanna snuffled about
in search of more fruit.

Jamie's heart sank as
he gazed up at the rock that towered above
him. The gingko trail had led them to the
mountains, but now they'd come to a dead
end and Wanna didn't seem to be able to
smell any more gingkoes. The pterosaurs
could have taken Tom miles away by now,
off to a high peak somewhere to be gobbled
up between them. Jamie couldn't bear to
think of such a thing happening to his friend.

He sat down despondently on a small boulder. Wanna trotted over to him and gently nudged his hand. He seemed to know that there was something wrong.

Jamie stroked the little dinosaur's head. 'You did your best, Wanna,' he told him. 'But I'm not sure what to do next.'

Then, to Jamie's surprise, Wanna suddenly trotted a little way off along the bottom of the cliff and began to make snuffling, slurping noises in the undergrowth.

'If I didn't know better I'd think you'd got another one of your favourite snacks!' said Jamie, going over to see what the little dinosaur had found. Wanna looked up—his snout was covered in gingko pulp!

Jamie gave a gasp of excitement. 'Brilliant, Wanna!' he yelled. 'You've sniffed out another clue. Tom must have come this way!'

CHAPTER 7

High up in the pterosaur nest Tom was looking desperately round for an escape route. If he tried climbing down the rock face he'd certainly fall to his death. The nearest tree, whose top was higher than the nest, was well out of reach—too far away for Tom to risk a jump.

The gingkoes I dropped could have been eaten straight away, he thought despairingly. *And without a trail to follow, Jamie and Wanna will never find me.*

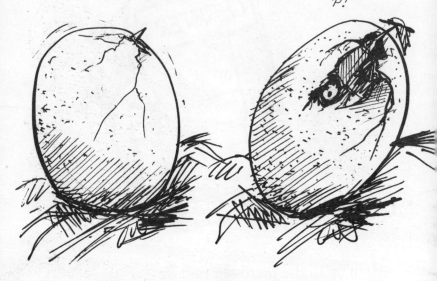

In the distance the two pterosaurs were circling the valley. Any minute now they could be back for their human feast.

Chip! Chip!

One of the huge eggs in the nest was moving and a crack ran across its surface. The crack grew wider and soon the tip of a beak could be seen hacking away at the shell. At last a big round eye appeared. For a moment Tom forgot his plight and watched,

fascinated, as a pterosaur
chick emerged, covered in slime
and pieces of eggshell. It wobbled on
two spindly legs and tried to shake the
shell off its sticky wings. It let out a high-
pitched squawk.

'Poor thing,' said Tom, picking the shell
from the chick's skin. Every time it saw his
hand moving it opened its mouth hungrily.
'Don't worry about food,' Tom told it bitterly.

85

'You'll probably be
nibbling bits of me later.'
As if it had understood,
the chick poked its beak at his
hand, squawking loudly.

'Shhh!' said Tom, scanning the skies.
'*You* might want to see your mum and dad,
but *I* certainly don't!'

Then Tom heard another sound. He
tensed and listened hard. No, he must have
been imagining it.

'TOM!' It was Jamie's voice. Tom looked
around wildly. 'Tom, where are you?'

Tom crawled to the edge of the precipice
and looked down. He couldn't believe
his eyes.

Far below him were Jamie and Wanna.
Jamie was waving and Wanna was trying in
vain to climb the cliff.

'I'm so pleased to see you!' yelled
Tom. 'I worried something would
have eaten the trail of gingkoes.'

'Something did eat them,' Jamie
yelled back. 'Guess who.'

Grunk!

'Good old Wanna!' shouted Tom.
'Now all I've got to do is get down from
here. Any ideas?'

Jamie pulled some long vines from
the massive tree growing closest to the
rock face.

'I'm coming to get you,' he called.

He coiled the vines
over his shoulder and
began the difficult
climb. The rough bark
grazed his knees. Halfway
up his foot slipped and
he felt the branch crack
below him. He shot out an
arm and clung on to a knot
in the trunk. He dangled
desperately trying to get
a foothold. At last he
wedged his toes into
the bark.

'Are you all right?' he heard Tom shout
in alarm.

'I'm OK!' he panted. 'Soon be there.'

After what seemed an age, he reached the
top branches and poked his head out to see
Tom grinning at him from the cliff ledge.

'Where's the backpack?' Jamie asked.

'I've got everything here,' Tom replied.
'Even the toffees! I know better than to leave
anything in Dino World.'

They could hear faint *grunks* from the
ground below.

'Wanna thinks we've abandoned him,'
said Jamie.

'Don't worry, boy,' Tom called down to the anxious little dino. 'We'll be back soon.'

'Cool!' exclaimed Jamie, catching sight of the pterosaur chick who was squawking loudly from its nest.

'As soon as its parents hear that racket they'll be down to feed it,' warned Tom. 'And we'll be pterosaur tea.'

'I've got an escape plan.' Jamie scrambled further up the tree. He looped the vine rope over a branch and tied one end firmly round his waist. 'Get ready to catch the other end,' he called, swinging it over to Tom.

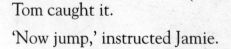

Tom caught it.

'Now jump,' instructed Jamie.

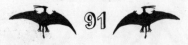

Tom looked down at the drop. 'I can't do it,' he said.

'There's no other way,' Jamie replied. 'You've got to jump.'

CAW!

The pterosaurs were back.

Tom jerked his head up. They were diving straight at them.

'You have to,' yelled Jamie. 'And right now!'

CHAPTER 8

Still clinging on to the vine tied around
Jamie's waist, Tom leapt off the ledge just as
the two flying serpents dived in to attack.
As he crashed into the spikey branches, he
caught a flash of their huge, sharp claws and
heard their angry cries. But he had made it to
the tree.

The boys scurried down the tree as quickly
as they could, and as soon as they reached
the ground Wanna grunked round them
in delight.

'Thanks for that, Jamie,' said Tom. 'Any time you're stuck in a pterosaur nest, waiting to be fed to its babies—I owe you one!'

There was a sharp cry overhead. Jamie looked up. 'Well, you don't have to wait long to repay me. The pterosaurs haven't given up.'

'Run!' shouted Tom. 'Make for the thickest trees. They won't be able to get us there.'

They dashed away down
the valley, following the river.
The pterosaurs screeched and
swooped above the forest, trying
to find a way through.

All of a sudden the
trees ahead gave way to low
undergrowth. And beyond
that—the open Plains.

'They'll snatch us up easily if
we go across there,' panted Jamie.

'There's no shelter.
But we can't stay here for ever.'
'Fancy a swim?' Tom pointed
towards the river. It rushed
down, white foam tumbling
against boulders and drifting tree
branches. 'I saw it from the air. It goes
off to the east but then it cuts back near
the jungle. It'll be fast but we're good
enough swimmers.'

'We'll be all right, but what about Wanna?' asked Jamie. 'He can't swim and we can't leave him to run along the bank. The pterosaurs will pick him off easily.'

'I've got it!' said Tom. 'We can make a boat for him, a sort of raft.' He began to gather some short fallen branches.

'Good idea,'
said Jamie, helping him.
'We can tie them together with vines.'

'Better be quick though.' Tom peered up through the leaves. The angry pterosaurs were circling right overhead.

Jamie nodded. 'We'll only have time to make it big enough for Wanna—and my backpack. We'll hang on to the edge and make sure he stays low.'

They lashed the branches together tightly with lengths of creeper.

'That should be big enough,' said Tom, leaning back on his heels and gazing at their rough craft. 'Let's hope it's riverworthy.'

They lifted it up and moved to the edge of the trees.

'Go for it!' yelled Jamie.

Holding the raft over their heads like a
shield, they made a dash for the riverbank,
Wanna scuttling underneath.

CAAAAW!

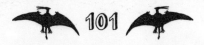

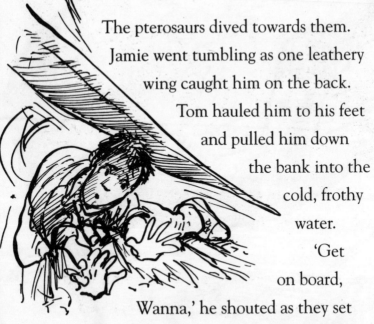

The pterosaurs dived towards them.
Jamie went tumbling as one leathery
wing caught him on the back.
Tom hauled him to his feet
and pulled him down
the bank into the
cold, frothy
water.
'Get
on board,
Wanna,' he shouted as they set
it afloat and held on tightly to stop it being
taken off by the strong current.

Wanna peered anxiously at the raft. Tom
put the backpack on it and fixed the strap
around the end of a log.

'You can do it, boy,' urged Jamie. The
pterosaurs were wheeling round for another
attack. 'The sooner we get back the sooner
you can have a nice gingko treat.'

But the little wannanosaurus backed away.
Suddenly there was a rush of air above him.

CAW!

A pterosaur was diving straight for his head.

Wanna took a running jump and landed
on the raft. It bobbed and bucked but kept
afloat. Wanna immediately flattened himself
in terror.

Jamie and Tom pushed off into the current and they sped along in the rough water. Their pursuers took to the sky, heading back for their nest. Now the danger was over, Wanna put his head up and grunked fiercely at them.

GRUNK!

'That's right, Wanna,' laughed Tom. 'See them off! We're not such easy targets now

we're moving so fast, and they've given up.
We're safe at last.'

'Not yet!' Jamie yelled back.

The raft was nearly snatched from their
hands. It spun and twisted, taking all their
strength to keep a grip.

'We've hit rapids,' spluttered Jamie. 'Hold
on tight.'

The raft thudded against rock after rock and shot down mini waterfalls of foam. The boys felt themselves tumbling helplessly in the current but they kept their hands clamped to the raft, knuckles white with the strain. Wanna watched everything silently.

After three little waterfalls and one bend, at last the river grew calmer.

'Wow!' gasped Tom. 'That was exciting. Though I feel a bit battered.'

'I've got bruises on my bruises,' laughed Jamie, looking over his shoulder.

'We've reached the Plains,' said Jamie, looking over at the bank.

'And after a while the river will bend back towards the jungle,' said Tom.

They let themselves be carried gently along, through the flat, dry landscape.

'We've seen no sign of any people,' said Jamie.

'And I've had an aerial view,' agreed Tom. 'Your dad must have been right. There must be another explanation for that professor's find.'

At last a wide curve of the river carried
them into a swampy area. They grabbed
a trailing root and pulled their makeshift
raft over to the bank. The hills rose ahead,
covered in the dark green of the trees. A short

climb and they'd be back at
the cave.

They climbed out,
helped Wanna off his
little boat, and began to
make their way across the
soft, muddy ground.

Tom took out his compass. 'I reckon we
need to go due west to get to Gingko Cave.'

'Sounds good to me,' said Jamie. 'Come
on, Wanna.'

They picked their way across the steamy
swamp towards the hills that rose up in front of
them. Their trainers squelched in the deep mud
as they tried to find patches of firm ground.

The sky was full of grey stormy clouds now and a fine rain began to fall.

'What's that?' gasped Jamie suddenly, pointing ahead at a strange mound he could just make out through the misty air.

'It's a dead dino,' said Tom as they got closer. 'Looks like a brachiosaurus.'

They walked round the gigantic body,
which lay between them and the trees.
Wanna hung back, sniffing the air anxiously.

'Wow!' exclaimed Tom, touching
the scaly skin. 'It's so huge.'

Grunk!

Wanna nudged at them as if he was
getting them to move away.

'Wanna seems scared,' said Jamie. 'It can't
hurt you, boy,' he told
the little
dinosaur.

At that moment they heard a deep, thunderous roar. They whirled round to see a herd of massive dinosaurs splashing across the swamp. The largest raised his head and roared again.

'Uh oh,' said Tom in a low voice. 'So that's what Wanna was trying to tell us.'

'Megalosaurs,' muttered Jamie. 'We're in trouble.'

CHAPTER 9

'Hide!' hissed Tom.

The boys dived behind a nearby conifer.

Trembling, Wanna pushed in between them. They crouched in their hiding place, watching through the spiky branches as the huge dinosaurs made for the brachiosaurus's body. The rain was falling steadily now, making swirling puddles of mud and splashing all about the carcass. With hungry roars, the massive creatures began to tear into the flesh.

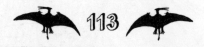

'We'd better sit it out until they've gone,' whispered Jamie. 'We can't risk being seen.' He looked up at the steep slope behind him. 'That's the way home but they'd be sure to spot us scrambling up there.'

Tom held an imaginary microphone to his mouth.

'And here we have the magnificent megalosaurs,' he whispered. 'These towering

predators have found an easy meal here in the swamp. The meggies are having a tasty brachiosaurus dinner.'

The megalosaurs were tearing off huge lumps of the scaly flesh, swallowing them down in greedy gulps and sinking their teeth in for more. They buffeted against each other to get to the meat.

'Wanna and I have already met one of these,' said Jamie wryly, 'and one was enough. We have to make sure they don't get wind of us.'

The largest megalosaurus was at the belly, taking the biggest share of the food. If any of others came near, he warned them off with deep rumbling growls. The others backed away nervously.

'That must be the leader,' whispered Tom. 'He certainly seems to be in charge.'

They watched as the leader ate his fill. The rain was getting heavier and the sky had grown dark and stormy.

'Perhaps this is a good time to make a move,' said Jamie, trying to stop the drips going down his neck. 'They may not see us now the light's so bad.' Then he noticed something moving through the swamp. 'What's that?' he whispered.

'It's another megalosaurus,' said Tom.

Now Jamie could see burning yellow eyes and a familiar battered face.

'Old Scarface,' he told Tom. 'That's the one Wanna and I had a close shave with before we found you. He can't be part of this herd or he'd have been with them when they arrived to eat.'

With a tremendous roar, the newcomer lurched towards the herd, whipping his head round on its powerful neck. He stared hungrily at the brachiosaurus meat, his mouth drooling.

Grunk!

Wanna seemed to remember the fierce dino from their earlier encounter. He turned to run

away, his paws scrabbling on the muddy slope.

'No, Wanna,' hissed Tom, grabbing a front leg and holding him firmly. 'It's too dangerous. Stay still.'

Scarface pounded towards the corpse. 'He's determined not to miss out on dinner,' said Jamie.

The head of the herd had raised his bloodstained snout to look at the interloper. He gave an answering roar, raised himself to his full height and snapped his jaws. Scarface bared his sharp teeth, thumping his tail hard on the ground.

The megalosaurs circled each other, heads high, snarling horribly.

'The leader's not going to let him get at their food,' said Tom. 'He sees this as a leadership challenge.'

'He's going to fight Scarface,' agreed Jamie.
'And that means a fight to the death.'

The rain was hammering down now,
splattering the two megalosaurs as they stalked
angrily around each other. The other dinosaurs
moved back to get out of the way of the fight.

'I've seen this sort of thing on television
with animals today,' whispered Jamie. 'The
herd follows the winner. They're impressed by
his strength and too scared to disobey.'

Scarface made the first move, slashing
at the leader with his fierce front claws.

His opponent gave an angry roar
as three bleeding slashes appeared
on his neck. He swung his
tail round, thumping into
Scarface and sending
him staggering
back.

The other megalosaurs grunted and stamped their feet.

'Scarface won't give up that easily,' whispered Jamie. 'He's a mean customer.'

Jamie was right. The newcomer suddenly lunged forwards, catching the leader by surprise and butting him hard in the chest. The leader retaliated by grabbing him with his front legs and biting down hard on his shoulder.

'Scarface looks badly injured,' said Tom. 'That gash is bleeding heavily.'

'He's still fighting though,' gasped Jamie as the battle-marked dino launched himself

again at the leader, churning up the red mud.

They locked together in a frenzy of claws and teeth. With an angry bellow, the leader threw Scarface off, making him reel back. He crashed into the tree where the boys and Wanna were hiding.

Then he shook himself and launched himself back down into the swamp, making for his enemy.

'That was close!' gasped Jamie.

CREAK!

They looked up to where the ominous noise was coming from. The trunk of the damaged conifer was splitting, throwing

splinters of bark into
the air.

Wanna gave an anxious
grunk.

'Uh-oh!' cried Tom.
'That tree's coming
down.'

'It's going to fall
on us!' yelled Jamie.
'Move!'

CHAPTER 10

Jamie, Tom, and Wanna dived out of the way as the thick tree trunk crashed to the ground. Tom cried out as a branch hit his face.

'Are you OK?' asked Jamie anxiously as they cowered next to the fallen conifer. Sticky yellow resin was leaking out from the trunk and oozing down to the ground.

Tom wiped his mouth and found a smear of blood on his hand. 'That hit me right in the jaw,' he answered, rubbing his jaw. 'It's not too bad but . . . oh!'

'What?' Jamie asked, sensing his friend's panic.

'Oh no!' Tom gasped and suddenly dived among the branches of the fallen trunk.

'What are you doing?' asked Jamie.

'That branch knocked out my loose tooth,' explained Tom. 'It's fallen out somewhere and I've got to get it back.'

'Leave it,' said Jamie urgently.

Tom turned to his friend, his fingers covered in the sticky resin.

'I can't,' he told him. 'I've just had a horrible thought. If my tooth has fallen in this stuff, it will become trapped in amber in millions of years' time. And you know what that means.'

Jamie gulped. 'That will be the tooth that the professor found in our time. He'll use it as proof that there *were* people around in the Jurassic era.'

'It will mess up all the dino timelines and everything,' Tom finished.

A huge megalosaurus foot stamped down on the branches by their heads. The two dinosaurs were still battling for leadership. Wanna grunked in alarm as he followed the boys up the slope to hide in some bushes.

'We'll have to leave the tooth,' panted Jamie. 'We've got no choice. I'd rather leave a tooth behind than have the fossilized hand we saw to be from one of us!'

The rain was a torrent now, causing rivulets to rush down the slope. The water carried soil and leaves from the higher ground, adding to the mud. They could hear distant thunder.

Heads down, the boys and Wanna clawed their way up the slope away from the roaring dinosaurs and the watching herd.

They suddenly
stopped and froze.
Through the driving rain
they could see two
megalosaurs in their
path—a mother and
her baby.

The mother had her
eyes fixed on the fight. Her
baby, no bigger than Wanna,
watched from behind a
cycad tree, its eyes
big and round
with fright.

'They haven't seen us,' said Jamie, as the
boys and Wanna edged sideways to avoid them.

'We'll have to take the long way round.'
Tom scoured the hills.

There was a rumbling sound on the slope
above and all of a sudden a wall of mud came
surging down towards the two dinosaurs,
sweeping up trees and boulders in its path.

'Landslide!' cried Jamie.

At the sight of the approaching mud slick
the mother megalosaurus gave a frightened
roar and bolted off towards the swamp.

Grabbing
Wanna between them,
the boys threw themselves clear
of the deadly avalanche of earth. When they
looked round they could see that a deep

mound of mud had built up around the cycad.
The baby was trapped up to its neck in the
middle of it.

It was making terrified calls and shaking its
head desperately. At last it pulled one front leg

free but that seemed to have exhausted it and it sank its head down on the sodden earth.

'We've got to do something,' said Jamie. 'We can't just leave it.'

The baby megalosaurus was writhing helplessly, trying to free itself as it sank further into the earth.

'It's calling for its mother again,' said Jamie. 'But she's too far away to hear.'

'It's up to us to free it then,' declared Tom. 'But without being seen. The minute any adult megalosaurs spot us we're dead meat.'

'Even the baby could attack us,' warned Jamie. 'We've never had to get a carnivore out of trouble before. We don't know how it'll react. But we've got no choice.'

He peered through the driving rain. Down below in the swamp, the herd had their eyes fixed on their leader and Scarface who were still battling away.

Followed closely by Wanna, the boys
waded into the thick mud of the landslide.

Tom slipped and fell, pulling Jamie with
him. The mud sucked at their hands and
feet as they tried to get up. At last, caked in
earth and wet through, they struggled to their
feet and clawed their way towards the baby.
Wanna scrambled after them, trembling with
fear at every roar of the gigantic beasts below.

Above the fury of the fight there was a
flash of light and a deafening crash of thunder.

'The storm's overhead,' cried Tom. 'There's
sure to be more
landslides
with all this
heavy rain.'

'We've
got to save
the baby
meggie now,'
shouted Jamie.

They had almost
reached the stranded baby
when one of the megalosaurs
whipped round, alerted
by their movement.
It let out a roar that
sent vibrations
through them.

The cry roused
the rest of the herd.
Heads turned, teeth
flashed, and an army of
massive legs started moving
up the slope towards the boys.

'Got to get away,' panted Tom,
tugging at Jamie's arm as the terrifying
megalosaurs surged towards them.

'We'll never move fast enough
through this mud,' gasped Jamie.

The huge carnivores
barged and snapped at
each other, each one
eager to be the first
to get to its prey.
Jamie, Tom,
and Wanna
shrank away from
the slavering jaws.
They were trapped.
Nothing could save
them from these
terrible monsters
now.

CHAPTER 11

Suddenly above their heads there was a tremendous rumbling as if an underground train was going to burst out from the hillside.

The rumbling grew louder and now Jamie and Tom could feel vibrations running through their feet and up their legs.

The megalosaurs stopped in their deadly approach.

Grunk!

Wanna's eyes were wide with terror.

'Look out!' yelled Jamie, pushing the little

dinosaur out of the way as a huge rock came bouncing down the side of the hill.

The megalosaurs gave petrified roars and stampeded away.

The baby squealed in panic, rocking its head from side to side and feebly waving its front leg.

'Come on,' cried Jamie. 'Before it's completely buried.'

They forced their way through the knee high mud and threw themselves at the mound of earth, scrabbling desperately to free the baby.

'Keep away from its mouth,' warned Jamie.

The little megalosaurus was snapping its sharp teeth in panic. The boys kept out of reach as they clawed at its earthy prison. At last they had uncovered the other front leg.

Grunk!

Wanna dug like a dog sending the mud spraying up behind him.

'It's working,' yelled Tom.

With a tremendous wriggle the baby broke free and bolted down the slope, crying for its mother.

'Brilliant!' exclaimed Jamie. 'We did it!'

'Time to get out of here,' shouted Tom. 'That scientist might have found my tooth but that's all he's going to find.'

There was a blinding flash of lightning followed by a rumble of thunder. But instead of dying away, the rumble seemed to be getting louder.

Jamie looked up, dashing the driving rain from his eyes.

143

'We've got to go NOW!' he bellowed.
'The whole side of the hill is coming down.'

They scrambled and slipped sideways out
of the path, Wanna darting ahead, using all
four feet to escape.

CRASH!

They were just in time. An avalanche
of mud and boulders tumbled down,
completely engulfing where they'd
been standing.

Tom and Jamie stood panting in the pelting rain.

'I'm glad we're not under that!' gasped Tom.

There was a crackle of breaking branches and suddenly a megalosaurus head poked out of the bushes nearby.

Grunk!

Wanna gave a warning cry.

'It's all right, boy,' gasped Jamie. 'It's the baby. I'm glad to see he made it out OK.'

The little megalosaurus made a small cry in its throat.

'He's saying thank you,' said Tom. He gave a bow. 'Not at all, youngster. It was our pleasure.'

'Just promise not to eat us if we meet again,' added Jamie.

'I don't think it works like that,' said Tom with a laugh.

The baby gazed solemnly at them for a moment, then turned and trundled off through the trees to find its mother.

'Race you back to the cave,' said Tom with a grin. 'We need to see that TV update and find out if they've discovered anything more about the tooth. I hope it was mine. Then we'll know there haven't been any other humans here.'

146

'Though I want to hear what they think about that hand,' replied Jamie. He burst out laughing. 'Can you imagine if they found a fossilized Fossil Finder!'

Wanna bounded ahead as the boys sprinted through the jungle and up the hill to Gingko Cave. Tom went over to a gingko tree and picked a handful of fruit.

'Here you are, boy,' he said, putting them on the ground and patting Wanna on his hard, domed head. 'This is a thank you for leading Jamie to the rescue.'

The little dinosaur settled down happily with his juicy snack.

The boys walked backwards in the footprints and soon found themselves in the smugglers' cave in Dinosaur Cove. As they made their way across the cave floor, the mud stains on their clothes and skin turned to dust.

'I wonder if the tooth fairy knows the way to Dino World,' said Tom with a grin. He prodded at the gap in his mouth with his tongue.

'You could always leave her a map under your pillow!' said Jamie. 'Though she'll have a

job. It'll be like looking for a pilchard in the ocean as Grandad always says.'

They stepped out into the sunshine and Jamie looked at their clothes.

'We can't go home like this,' he said. 'We're covered in Jurassic dust!'

'A quick dip in the sea first
then,' suggested Tom. The boys
scrambled down over the rocks,

sneaked across the beach and plunged into
the sea to wash themselves clean. Then they
sprinted up to the lighthouse and burst into
Dad's office just as the newsflash was starting.

The reporter was outside the cave again.

'We come back to you with breaking news,'
he told the camera. 'Experts have examined the
tooth and agreed it is indeed human. It's a milk
tooth, probably from a child of about nine.'

'I don't believe it!' gasped Dad. 'There
can't have been humans in the Jurassic age.'

Jamie and Tom tried not to look at each other.

'I have Professor Jenkins here with me now,' the reporter went on. The camera swung to show the scientist, rocking on his heels and looking very pleased with himself. 'There's a bit more to the report, Professor. Perhaps you could explain what it means to our viewers.'

The scientist looked puzzled.

'The fossilized hand has also been examined,' said the reporter coldly. 'It's a fake! What have you got to say about that?'

'Well . . . it's . . . ' the professor spluttered.

'It's made up of the bones from a gibbon and an orang-utan,' said the reporter. 'And it's only about forty years old. And as for the tooth. It might be real and I'm told that the amber round it certainly was very old but the experts are working on how you pulled off that stunt.' He turned back to the screen. 'So there you have it. There were no humans alive two hundred and fifty million years ago. I'm afraid this will go down in history as the Bogus Bones of Bridwell Bay.'

Professor Jenkins was bright red in the face. 'OK, I admit it; I made up the hand fossil,' he blustered. 'But the tooth's genuine. It really is. I found it right here, in amber in the rock.'

'If the tooth's genuine,' snapped the reporter, 'how do you explain the traces of toffee found on it. Are you saying there were sweet shops back in the Jurassic?'

Jamie and Tom burst out laughing.

Dad switched the TV off.

'What a fool that man was,' he said. 'Can you imagine it—humans in the world of the dinosaurs! Impossible.'

Jamie and Tom looked at each other and grinned. Only they knew how 'impossible' it really was!

DINOSAUR WORLD

- - - - BOYS' ROUTE

✗ WHERE TOM IS SNATCHED BY PTEROSAURS

Humongous Waterfall

Massive Canyon

Plains

Fin Rock ◁

Jurassic Ocean

GLOSSARY

Allosaurus (al-oh-sor-us) – one of the largest meat-eating dinosaurs and one of the fiercest predators of its time. Its name means 'different lizard' because its backbone was shaped differently than other dinosaurs.

Archaeopteryx (ar-kee-op-ter-ix) – small bird-like feathered creature, capable of flight. It had sharp teeth, three clawed fingers, a long bony tail, and a second toe for use as a 'killing claw'. Archaeopteryx was not a fussy feeder, eating small animals, plants, and insects.

Brachiosaurus (bra-kee-oh-sor-us) – had a long neck, like a giraffe. This gentle giant loved its greens, munching through around 150 kgs of plants a day!

Camarasaurus (cam-ah–roh-sor-us) – a long-necked, long-tailed giant herbivore with spoon-shaped teeth and a hollow backbone.

Cretaceous (cret-ay-shus) – from about 65 to 150 million years ago, this time period was home to the widest variety of dinosaur and insect life of any period. Birds replaced winged dinosaurs, while in the sea, sharks and rays multiplied.

Cycads (si-kads) – plants with thick trunks, palm-like leaves, and cones.

Diplodocus (dip-lod-oh-kus) – one of the longest land dinosaurs with a long-neck and whip-like tail. This huge dinosaur had pencil-shaped blunt teeth perfect for its plant-only diet.

Gingko (gink-oh) – a tree native to China called a 'living fossil' because fossils of it have been found dating back millions of years, yet they are still around today. Also known as the stink bomb tree because of its smelly apricot-like fruit.

Jurassic (jur-as-sick) – from about 150 to 200 million years ago, the Jurassic age was warm and humid, with lush jungle cover and great marine diversity. Large dinosaurs ruled on land, while the first birds took to the air.

Megalosaurus (meg-ah-loh-sor-us) – a large meat-eating dinosaur of the Jurassic Period. It was the first dinosaur to be discovered and named.

Pterosaur (ter-oh-sor) – a prehistoric flying reptile. Its wings were leathery and light and some of these 'winged lizards' had fur on their bodies and bony crests on their heads.

Stegosaurus (steg-oh-sor-us) – a large plant-eating dinosaur. It had heavy plated armour and a long row of kite shaped spikes down its spine, and another row behind its shoulders for defence.

Wannanosaurus (wah-nan-oh-sor-us) – a dinosaur that only ate plants and used its hard, flat skull to defend itself. Named after the place it was discovered: Wannano in China.